EMILEE
ANONYMOUS

BY
F.A. CARROLL

Emilee Anonymous by: F.A. Carroll

Copyright © 2015 Double D Publishing

www.FACarroll.com

DEDICATION

My achievements have been few, yet still, I dedicate this story to all of the kids I consider my own

(Alyssa – Anthony – Riley) - My actual three –

Chance Nelson, William Carroll, Hailey Roberts, Mikayla McLaughlin, Ryan McLaughlin, Melissa Jagrosse, Kaitlyn Krasny, Kailee Desiderio and all of the friends of my children.

My awesome nieces and nephews

Jake, Samantha and Alex Rainsdon

Lucy, Levi and Noah Edvalson

And to my newest love

Kylie Smithgall

A special thank you to Neira Garcia for her name

And to my fellow Author, friend, and role model, Dr. Richard Selzer.

I wish I met you sooner. I love everything you are. Thank you for reading everything that I have written. Thank you for telling me when I sucked.

PREFACE

Emilee, the story, began as a thought of where we end up when we die. The names, and the events are fictional, but the story is a graphic depiction.

Suicide is a serious dilemma and a choice often made during dire, yet correctable circumstances. I have known people who have attempted suicide, and many have unfortunately succeeded.

This book came close to remaining unfinished when a dear friend lost her Son. After contemplating it, I reached out to my friend. Without a pause, she gave me her blessing to continue writing.

This is not a pro-suicide book. It is a harsh reality of the loved ones left behind.

This book contains graphic nature.

If you or anyone you know needs assistance, please **DO NOT** hesitate to contact the National Suicide Hotline.

1-800-273-8255

www.suicidepreventionlifeline.org

PROLOGUE

"Happiness is a small and unworthy goal for something as big and fancy as a whole lifetime, and should be taken in small doses."
—Russell Baker

"Life is one big road with lots of signs.
So when you riding through the ruts, don't complicate your mind.
Flee from hate, mischief and jealousy.
Don't bury your thoughts, put your vision to reality.
Wake Up and Live!"
—Bob Marley

Suicide sometimes proceeds from cowardice, but not always; for cowardice sometimes prevents it; since as many live because they are afraid to die, as die because they are afraid to live.
Charles Caleb Colton

The more often we see the things around us - even the beautiful and wonderful things - the more they become invisible to us. That is why we often take for granted the beauty of this world: the flowers, the trees, the birds, the clouds - even those we love. Because we see things so often, we see them less and less.

Joseph B. Wirthlin

CHAPTER ONE
"Life is but a thought."
(Coleridge)

At one point in my life, I have written two bestselling novels. *On the Edge of Seventeen*, my debut, and *Raising Riley*, have both reached number one on the New York Times bestsellers list and both are available in multiple languages. I have won numerous awards for my literary and humanitarian efforts, all while receiving positive reviews for both my style and genre. The business of writing used to praise my success.

"Robert H. Bramwell, if the words he wrote were oxygen, with his the world could breathe." (Richard Selzer -The Man behind the Story. *Writers Inc. Magazine*

August 1999: page 23. Print.)

If you met me today, you wouldn't believe this. I hardly believe it myself. After years of anonymity, the world moved on without me. I'm a shadow of my old self, a broken and lost version so fragile and empty, with little desire to live. My family has given up on me (although I don't blame them) – no one remains.

My closest friends are the ghosts that fill my mind. They rarely leave me alone, and I always know when they're near. They speak directly to me, hidden in the darkness, lurking, whispering softly until I nearly go insane.

"Do it, Robert. Do it…" But I never do.

I don't know if I can take much more, although I don't know how to end it. I'm drowning every day, slowly from the inside out. This medicated, pathetic life, which I, admittedly, self-created, has become a full-blown addiction.

I have heard life is what you make of it and I've made mine of shit.

My name is Robert and I'm an alcoholic. This is my first attempt at writing in over three years.

***

9 August

No matter how many times I have tried to erase it, the event and the result never die. With all of my efforts, it remains the one thing on my mind. It was the final day, her final moment. I just can't forget, and it haunts me every minute.

***

Every night that I was home — I watched Neira sleep. Often leaning against her bedroom doorframe while sipping my evening cocktail and erasing my day away. This bedtime moment inspired me every night. Just seeing her perfect, round face eliminated the fatigue. She was perfect to me.

I'd admire how her tiny fingers clutched her tattered blanket to her chest, and how it rose with every breath. And how her hair rested perfectly still on the pillow while she dreamt sweetly, so peaceful and picturesque. At times she would speak. Her words usually made little sense, but they were from her, and so I listened.

On other nights, for a moment so slight, she would giggle. An innocent response to what she may have been dreaming. It always made me smile. A need to steal one more kiss would come over me, and so I would.

First, I removed my shoes, placing them side by side outside her bedroom door. While trying not to wake her, I'd tiptoe across the floor, maneuver past all of her scattered toys around my feet like a soldier in a minefield. Her eyes always opened as I approached, sensing my presence. They always reclosed with a simple kiss on the bridge of her nose. It was magical. It was always a special moment.

I'd sit on the edge of her bed until I knew she was back to sleep, stroking her hair, brushing it away from her perfect face until her gentle snore resumed. It never took long. Before leaving, I would place one last loving kiss on her cheek and then tiptoe away in the dark.

I'm unsure if she ever knew I did this and unsure if she ever will. She's gone.

I miss her gently placed kisses and her crooked little mouth. The way the dimple on her left cheek deepened with the width of her smile. I miss her hands resting over my face, touching my stubble, massaging the skin before nuzzling me, cheek to cheek.

Her kisses before going to bed were simply the best. It began with the patter of footy pajamas sliding on the wood floor. That always let me know she was on her way.

I'd pretend I didn't know she was behind me and continue typing. She'd sneak up on me while shushing my wife with her full voice. Of course, I could hear her, but the innocence in the moment made it all that more memorable. I'd whip around before she grabbed me and swoop her into my arms. That's when the tickle monster attacked her weak spots until she begged me to stop.

We did this every night, until she stopped at around age ten. After begging me to stop, she would hug me tight. Her voice softly whispering in my ear, "Nigh' nigh' Dada. Nigh' night."

It's impossible to explain what it feels like to lose a child. The best I could say is the words meant the world, but it's the kisses I miss the most. It's never feeling her skin pressed gently against my face. It's her as a whole — laughing, smiling, and making me do the same.

I regret taking the routine for granted, and thinking it could never end. I regret not being there to save her when she needed me most.

***

Every so often, she appears from out of nothing, dancing with a child-like innocence across my kitchen floor. Her hair pulled back perfectly in a low pony, and her face concealed with enough stage makeup to add ten years to her age. I always buy into the moment, sit up from my drunken slouch and give my full attention. Her never-ending smile stretches cheek-to-cheek and it never leaves her face.

She taps her tiny feet against the tile floor, raising her hands to her lips while blowing kisses toward my face. I pretend to catch them in my fists and store them in my pocket. That always made her smile. It still does.

Flawlessly, she ends the routine without a hitch, bends her knee with an unbalanced curtsy, smiles, and waves goodbye. I beg her to stay — I plead for her to speak with me but she never does. In a flash, she disappears just as quickly as she appeared. The room goes dark. And the shadows return.

Nevertheless, she isn't actually here. It's merely a drunken mirage I made up in my mind. They're the memories locked away deep down inside which emotionally trigger unwillingly. Her kisses never find my face and my happiness fades away. On one hand, I'm happy to endure the pain of being able to see her. On the other hand, I could live without it. Although the choice isn't mine to make.

***

It took me a long time to accept her death as self-inflicted. When her mother had finally found her she had died on her bedroom floor. With a short, hand written note crumpled in a ball beside her, and an empty pill bottle resting loosely in her lifeless hand. There was never a chance to save her.

We'd never seen signs of her being upset or depressed. Her social life appeared active and we provided her with anything she needed. Her grades were average, but the teachers always spoke positively about her personally, often commenting on her ability to write.

I believed in her, but I was always too busy. My life, my next book, my traveling for my fans always took center stage.

We never recognized the cries for help. She always smiled. Now I question whether the smile was real, or if I missed any false grins that she gave me in passing. But I will never know, and I will never forgive myself for it.

***

I was at a meet and greet for *Raising Riley* when the call finally reached me after several failed attempts. I rushed home, leaving my fans with no explanation. I never knew what was happening beyond a major medical presence at my house. My mind raced through scenarios, none of them correct, and all of them tragic.

I pulled into the driveway, parked my car beside the emergency vehicles and ran into my house. Being an author of marginal fame, the sidewalk photographers got to the scene ahead of me. Honestly, in the moment, I didn't even give them a thought. They failed to profit in that moment.

A female officer initially stopped me at the doorway, but a detective at the top of the stairs rushed down them once he recognized who I was.

"Let him by," he said.

An antiquated well-dressed detective stood in front of me. His eyes locked on mine with a serious expression on his face. Our hands embraced business like but he never let go. Instead, he drew me toward him, obstructing my view. His seriousness never changed.

"What's going on here?" I said.

"Sir, Mr. Bramwell, — I'm Detective Nelson"

I grew uncomfortable and stepped back, pulling my hand from his while attempting to look over his shoulder. Detective Nelson's demeanor and rehearsed greeting hadn't satisfied my negative thoughts. In fact, it enraged them further.

"Please calm down sir. Let me explain."

"Where's my wife?" I demanded.

"She's upstairs, she's fine."

"What happened then? I need to see her."

Taking charge, the detective slapped down his large hands on my shoulders, He looked directly into my eyes.

"I'm sorry Mr. Bramwell… it's your daughter."

I pushed past him before he finished speaking. Considering my rudeness, he didn't try to stop me as I rushed up the stairs, passing emergency workers who blocked my path. I pushed myself between two officers blocking her doorway.

Then my world went cold. I froze where I stood.

She lay there motionless – surrounded by strangers. A limp body folded on the floor like a paper doll discarded. A white sheet placed over her head hid her face from me, but I knew it was Neira.

I broke down, falling beside my daughter's lifeless body, and cried. I cried and I pleaded. Never believing in God, I began to pray – I don't know why.

He never arrived.

My wife stood staring out the bedroom window, inconsolably sobbing. Two officers did their best to comfort her but the hurt was just too much. The media outside in the street aimed their lenses and chose this photo opportunity. They used it to profit. And I will never forgive them.

The detectives tried moving me away but I resisted. I had to stay beside her, holding her hand like when she was a little girl. Only now her hand didn't grip mine back. It felt loose and cold. Nothing was there. I raised it to my mouth and warmed it with my breath, kissed it, and nuzzled it against my cheek while choking back tears, "Wake up - please baby girl wake up." But my Neira never awoke.

Eventually weakening, I got up from the floor, placing her hand on her stomach before walking away. It was too late to save her, so I went to my wife and held her. We cried, clutched together, falling to pieces in each other's arms.

The hours passed. The response team dispersed one by one. Detective Nelson let us have a moment alone with Neira before removing her body. We appreciated the opportunity and it was hard to say goodbye. Both of us held her hands while singing a nursery rhyme she loved when she was little. We spoke to her lovingly. I would rather keep the moment unwritten and between my wife, myself and our child.

Within hours, I went from a book signing success to a childless father and failure.

My wife surrounded herself in the dark that night, crying herself to sleep in our child's bed — alone. I chose to get drunk until passing out, doing nothing to console her. We never even spoke – or maybe I never listened. Either way I failed — not only her, but our daughter too.

CHAPTER TWO
"Love comes unseen; we only see it go."
(Austin Dobson)

The funeral came and went. I lashed out at anyone attempting to soothe me while medicating excessively with a doctors blessing. I began drinking to forget, hiding all my feelings behind a closed door. My wife eventually tired of my antics and our marriage dissolved. She moved on, and far away. I hear she's doing well. We haven't spoken since.

They all disappeared. In less than one year's time every friend, loved one and relative stopped checking in. My writing career ended. I just didn't care. Everyone went on with his or her life while I grieved alone, drunk and defeated, fixating on finding the answers to why Emilee took her life. I threw pity parties every night. With every breath inhaled, the exhale carried guilt. I missed my daughter every second, and with passing years, the pain never lessened.

***

Three long years, still nothing had changed. My finances were thinning as the publisher's lawsuits piled up. The dullness of my days and the repetitive vision of Neira choking, slowly dying, aided in the decision. I needed to die. My body and mind had both agreed. I woke every morning considering suicide, and even weakly attempting to do it several times, but failed. On this day, I was courageous. The very thing that destroyed my life had now become desirable. An absolute obsession, believing I could see her again, overrode my rational. I wanted to die. And I wanted to die today.

OUR STORY BEGINS - An August night.

A constant rain tapped on the window beside my chair. Sudden flashes of lightning lit up the room, while bone-shaking blasts of thunder shook the floorboards beneath my feet. None of it fazed me. My thoughts were wandering elsewhere as they often do.

My daily routine of misery mixed with gin had escalated far from its normal form. As usual, I started mid-morning and continued to drink throughout the day. One bottle usually numbed me, but I had a specific plan. A second bottle would push me toward my goal.

I carefully navigated the hallway, staggering and using the wall as support until finding my office door. I entered. The room resembled a ghost town settled in dust. A lot of unused research I had boxed up was scattered throughout the room — each one stacked upon the other and collapsing under the pressure. I maneuvered around them.

After opening the closet door and moving binders of family photos, there it was, high up on the shelf and just out of reach. A dull, dusty, gray lockbox tucked neatly beside a box of Christmas bulbs.

I rolled my swivel chair to the wall, balanced as if agile, grabbed it, and then stepped off. Blowing off the dust-covered handle before gripping it like a lunch box and stumbling back down the hall — unharmed.

Sitting back in my chair, placing the gray metal lockbox beside me, I opened it. The hinges screamed and deposited a small pile of fine rust on the table. Without much struggle, it opened to reveal a pistol. It nestled tightly into a foam insert with a full round of bullets beneath it. A small notepad with a pen prepacked, rested neatly ready to go.

"Only a dramatic writer would prepare a suicide kit," I said smiling.

I plucked each bullet from the foam holder, and placed each one methodically on the table beside me. Six stood tall in a row reflecting the flickering candle on the table, while daring me with their glare.

I picked up the pistol, twisting it in my hand before positioning it between the bump in my throat and the thin skin beneath my jaw. The steel tip of the pistol was cold, so I pulled away. One deep, relaxing swallow put the pistol back in place. I began pulling the trigger in between breathes, practicing my kill shot. I knew then and know now — I was letting fear control the moment. I had never fired a gun in my life. Actually, I take that back, that's not true. I never loaded one before.

***

When I was a child, I found it buried in my mother's dresser drawer, far back in the corner beneath the socks and boxer briefs my father had left behind. My mom had no clue I'd found it, and most likely had no idea it was there. I always examined its exact location and returned it just the same.

The gun looked enormous in my small hands. When I aimed it, I felt so strong and powerful. I thought I was a cop from one of my television shows. Whipping my head around, pointing the weapon, snarling into the mirror, pretending I had cornered a criminal who had no escape.

One Saturday morning, while my mother worked an extra shift, I went to play cop. She rarely left me alone. However, after I showed her some responsibility she decided four hours on my own would be fine. What could a twelve year-old boy possibly do?

"Drop your weapon," I said with the deepest voice I could muster. "Halt dirt bag – freeze... or else," while aiming at my own reflection in my mother's antique mirror.

I pulled back the trigger making gunshot sounds while firing. *Bang, bang...Bang, bang...*, then staring down at my make believe thief who was lying wounded on the ground.

"Picked the wrong cowboy," I said before laughing like a lunatic, tilting my head back and removing my dark glasses. I pointed the gun for the kill shot, smiled and winked, locked on my target, and then pulled the trigger.

BOOM!

Glass shattered. The gun flew from my hand. The kick back sent me flying through the air, dropping me like a ragdoll on the bed. I laid there in shock, catching my breath. I was frantic. Everything happened so quickly my mind couldn't comprehend.

I rolled off the bed, checking my body for any harm — no blood.

The gun had come to rest by my feet. A puff of grey smoke exhaled from its barrel and the smell of rotten eggs filled the room. I tried to pick up the gun, but dropped it back down in an instant when it burned my hand. I shook the heat from my fingers, blowing feverishly on them before wrapping my hand in my sleeve, grabbing the gun, and tossing it into the drawer, slamming it shut.

The mirror's glass was everywhere. I ran to the hall and returned with a vacuum, plugged it in, and began to clean my mess. Every sweep sounded like loose change sucking in.

I covered the hole in the wall with duct tape hoping she wouldn't notice. (Remember I was twelve.)

When my mother came home, I sat in front of the television watching *Scooby Doo* and acting *normal*, sweating from fear on the inside.

It didn't take very long for her to notice. The volume of her voice let me know when she had. "Robert James Bramwell", echoed through the house with an emphasis on my middle name. I knew I was in big trouble.

"Get your ass in here...NOW!" she shouted, not to mention cursed. Possibly the only time I have ever heard her swear.

***

I suffered a brutal consequence. Her punishment was harsh and painful. All of my remaining summer days locked in my bedroom without any source of pleasure. No fun, just books – the long and boring classics with words that I still don't understand. She expected a long form essay on them all. It seemed never ending. At the time, I thought it was extreme, but now I understand her reasoning.

She claimed to have no knowledge of a gun being in the dresser. She soon after sold it to our neighbor, or so I thought, and so she said.

I was nineteen years old when she passed. She never was able to see my success. Upon turning twenty-one, my Uncle Robert, her brother, delivered a shiny, gray box with a note attached.

My dearest boy,

Although not funny, in fact extremely dangerous, your antics on that day must have been worthy of filming. How you must have jumped from your skin. Remember always to check the chamber before handling. This gun is all I can offer from your father.

Love you to the moon and beyond,
Mom XOXO

I have never fired it since. I bought ammo and had it appraised, but like my father, it was worthless.

***

I channeled my courage after wasting an hour with practice. Lit a final cigarette, picked up the gun and playfully spun the chamber — just to watch it spin. Refocusing, I loaded one bullet. Clicked back the hammer, released the safety, exhaled, and positioned my finger on the trigger. I pressed the barrel beneath my chin. My hand shook violently but settled the harder I pushed. My eyes slammed shut. I began the end of my life with a slow count of three.

One – Two – Thr...
BANG – BANG – BANG

CHAPTER THREE
"Ambition is the last refuge of the failure."
(Oscar Wilde)

The silence shattered. My eyes popped open wide. I dropped the gun to the floor and gave my full attention down the hallway. Three loud knocks from the front room echoed through my church-silent home.

Was it the storm, or, on the other hand, a tree branch slapping the windows in the breeze? I wasn't sure and I really didn't care to know. I was frightened. My heart pounded in my chest as if a caged animal trapped inside me were trying to escape.

I stood up, grabbing the gun from the floor. After placing it on the table beside the remaining bullets, I froze, standing statuesque and focused, prepared to run if needed. Three more knocks - loud and solid.

KNOCK – KNOCK – KNOCK.

At first, between my drunken condition and my fear, I didn't recognize them as door knocks. It never entered my thoughts until the storm door springs squeaked in the wind.

"Who's there?"

Like a terrified child with a fear-filled, weak and empty voice. What I had shouted in my head came out of my mouth as a whisper. I tried again, over compensating, screaming with all my effort.

"Who's there?"

No answer returned. My own voice echoed back. The wind shook the windows glass, sending shivers through my bones.

I stepped toward the hallway, cupped my ear with my hand for a closer listen. Trying not to lose my balance, I used the wall. Thirty seconds passed – no knocks, no sounds.

Knock – knock…Knock.

My fears became anger. I began shouting incoherently, increasing my volume with every word.

"Who is there?" "Hello, answer me – damnit."
The knocking returned.

Knock – knock – knock, a short pause and then, knock – knock – knock, repeatedly without ending.

My mentality was fragile. The constant knocking echoed like a pickaxe inside my brain, attempting to breakout above my eyes. I was angry, drunk and unstable. So used to being alone that any interruptions to my time set me off. I stammered my way through obscenities, steadied my feet, and pushed away from the wall. While grabbing at the gun, I spilled the bullets on the floor, along with the last of my gin.

***

While bouncing through the living room and knocking over everything in my path, I leaned over the sofa, moving the drapes enough to see through the front bay window. A person, female, judging by size, stood facing the door beneath the eave. Her bright yellow, hooded raincoat hid her face, but she wasn't hiding, at least not from me. The knocks strengthened.

My anti-social lifestyle brought a panic to me like a heroin addict with a missing spoon. I continued toward the door, took three deep breaths to gather my head, turned on the porch light and grasped the knob. The knocks had stopped.

I swung open the door prepared to shout, "WHAT?", but no one was there. The knocker was gone. I watched from the doorway with a slight smile on my face as she walked away, Stepping undeterred on my flooded walkway, unafraid, and never looking back. Her car door opened, she got in and drove off without any care. I waved like a drunken beauty queen, still swaying side to side.

"Thanks for stopping by." I laughed to myself.

"Please come again."

***

I began to shut the door before it caught my eye. A dark colored backpack leaning against the lamppost with the light above reflecting off its silver emblem. I scooped it up. Caught my balance after underestimating its weight, and took a quick look around before heading back inside.

Stumbling back through the living room by following the debris like a trail of crumbs, I tossed the backpack on the table, and shook the excess water from my skin. Then I saw the empty gin bottle with its contents puddled up on the kitchen floor. I bent to one knee beside it and ran my hand through the spill, licking my fingers as a cat licks its paw.

Then all went black.

CHAPTER FOUR
"Hope is a waking dream."
Aristotle

I awoke on the kitchen floor with the sun shining through the kitchen window, directly into my eyes. My head pounded and the light didn't help. I rolled over to eliminate the sun and then jumped to a sitting position as a bullet point stabbed me in the back.

"Try to put it through my head and instead impale my spine," I said, rubbing away the pain.

My head was foggy, my memory the same. I struggled to remember not only why there were bullets scattered on the floor but also why a puddle of gin. The gears in my brain began to move. I grabbed at the kitchen table and lifted my weary body to the chair. The backpack on the table sped up the gears.

My hangover left me with a sharp knocking which pulsed like a heartbeat above my right brow. I wanted to vomit. My mouth was dry and I desperately needed a drink. The back of my throat burned as if I had swallowed a lit book of matches, yet still I craved a cigarette.

I tried to remember my night while burying my face in my palms and taking deep breaths. The endless knock above my left eye prevented me from focusing clearly. I feverishly pressed my thumbs into my eye socket just at the bridge of my nose. Temporarily, the pain subsided, but returned within seconds more intense. My fingertips explored my skull, pushing into the pain zones between pulsating throbs. Nothing worked. Then snap! – I remembered the knocking.

Each part of the night returned, foggy and broken, eventually falling together like a puzzle where the pieces are unfocused. My chest burned. I went to the sink and poured a large glass of water. After a brief struggle with the safety cap, four Advil travelled harshly down my throat. I refilled my glass, grabbed a fifth of gin from the cabinet, before collapsing back into my drinking chair.

The backpack stared back at me. My headache subsided. Water droplets from the previous night's storm still fell from its zippers tab, puddling in a small divot in the table before flowing over the edge, and onto the floor. I grabbed it by its strap and placed it on the floor beside me. After unzipping it, and peering curiously inside, I considered it safe.

Several wrapped packages were crammed tightly against the sidewalls, nearly splitting the seams of the backpack. I stuck my arm in and removed the contents. Once empty, I felt around for anything I may have missed. A hand written index card, still wet from sitting in the rain, and barely legible, rested on the bottom of the bag. I pulled it out.

Robert-Bramwell
22 Acacia Avenue
Branford CT 06405

I tore open the packages. My interest had been piqued. I threw the wrapping debris to the floor in different directions like a kid on Christmas day. Each package had a stack of single subject notebooks- every color, college ruled. All of them dated in the top left corner.

A yellow notebook labeled **EMILEE,** written boldly in a thick black marker caught my eye.

- I opened it.

(*We never speak – we never fight – we never discuss my day.
She is here though – I can hear her – but I rarely see her.
    If I dressed as a prescription bottle for Halloween, I may attract her attention. She would swallow me whole.
(Jokes on her though, because I'm empty.)
    Am I at all transparent?
There I am, leaning over the edge. Does anybody see me?*

*NOTE TO SELF: NEXT YEARS COSTUME —
Prescription pad…
    She will have no choice but to refill me… it's what she does the best.*) <u>EMILEE</u>

***

Over the next few hours, I read her notes. Her depressing words were emotional and honest; dark passages from a girl whose depression had driven her mad. Emilee was her name, and it was her backpack left on my doorstep. Why, I can't explain. We've never met.

She bounced between pages of in depth detail and sporadic quotes. Often following events with well thought out doodling which was both dark, and at times, humorous. Her timeline set between the ages of ten until the eve of her sixteenth birthday. Every page filled with enough information to tell her story.

(I wonder if the world can go on without me.

I guess they would have to know that I exist. Today I was called a misfit. It's hard to argue with the truth.) <u>EMILEE</u>

***

The day flew by and the nighttime crept in, but I never noticed. For the first time in several years I felt clear minded and sober. I never had a sip of alcohol that day and haven't since.

The bottom notebook was blue. The cover said, "FOR YOU", in a thick black permanent marker. I opened it.

Mr. Bramwell,

These notebooks contain my life. They possibly will help you with yours.

I know you are/were a writer. Write my story.

"Nate told me it was time."

Em

"Nate? My daughter…, It couldn't be, could it?"

I spun in my chair; rubbing my tired eyes while watching the darkness creeping in. My insides ached. The sun disappeared beyond the tree line and a peace I feared lost forever came over me. I smiled. I hadn't smiled in some time.

"No one outside this house knew I called her Nate."

I went into my office, cleaned up my desk and neatly stacked her notebooks on the edge, before sitting down. I became her choice. I didn't need to know why. (Although I desperately wanted answers), Somehow, "Nate" was sending a message; it had to be enough for me to try.

Once again, with a purpose and a goal I was a writer.

CHAPTER FIVE
"He, who doesn't fear death, dies only once."
Giovanni Falcone

October

(It is usually impossible to describe the feeling of hanging. In fact, it is virtually unheard of in most cases. Receiving a second chance in life is so rare and unlikely you have to consider it a gift.

Whether you believe in God and the gift is from him, or plain shit luck actually gave you a reprieve, take that gift and re-evaluate. Suicide may remove you successfully from the living, temporarily solving the issue at hand, but trust me, where it takes you is not HEAVEN...)

EMILEE

***

She sat on her bed, staring through her window watching the wind blow away all of the clouds. In that moment she imagined how easy life would be if a simple breeze could push away all of the pain. If the dark clouds surrounding her were suddenly gone, would it matter? She didn't believe it would, but it was all she had known. After years of invisibility, the clouds had become part of her life. She knew she'd be lost without them.

These were the harsh years of high school. Emilee never fit in. Her simplistic sense of style and unattractive looks (according to her) had cast her aside from the cliques.

At home, she was invisible. In the classroom, she remained the same. Whenever she did try to fit in the kids only laughed, eventually she just stopped caring. The lack of parental support to help her deal with any problems beat Emilee down through the years. She became isolated. Over the following years depression set in. No one recognized her pain. No one ever asked.

The day-to-day grind was tiring. Like a repetitive carousel spinning uncontrolled, no matter how loud she screamed. Her schoolwork faltered - no consequence. The teachers quit. Only music and writing got her through each day.

(He walked past me again today. He never said hello.
Did he forget I'm here? Did he forget about his
daughter?)
EMILEE

Emilee struggled with being alone. Surviving unnoticed and invisible while the two people who created her argued endlessly in the room next door. A mother who at one time had cared with an overbearing desire, stayed in bed all day. Often, so high on prescriptions, that she forgot whom Emilee was. She quit as a parent, and quit as a person. She became a pathetic skeleton of pale skin. Her soul destroyed - poisoned by doctors who fed her inner demons. Pills replaced Emilee and acquiring them became her job.

Her father was weak and beaten. He couldn't figure things out on his own and did the minimum to provide care for Emilee. Instead, he chose to save his wife from the flames she had lit, as his innocent child choked on the smoke, and burned in the room beside them.

It had to end.

**

(Some call me names and others only stare directly through me.
I'm not beautiful or athletic. I'm not remotely interesting enough to fit into any clique.
Maybe I'm invisible, maybe I don't matter at all.
Maybe once I go away someone may miss me. Maybe no one will care at all. Who knows?
The pain may not show on my face and my silence may make you think I am fine, but I'm not.
I'm broken. How sad I have to die to be remembered at all.)
EMILEE

Emilee had needs that no one at home assisted. She had trouble maintaining any true friendships because bringing them home was an embarrassment. Her mother would wander the house in a fog, high off her ass, mumbling incoherently and lost in her own home. Often her face bruised from falling, and at times barely dressed. She was disgusting.

It didn't take long before the other kids' parents would forbid them from going over. Could you blame them?

The home was a disaster. Wall holes patched so often they resembled scars. Piles of unwashed dishes rose from the sink and spilled out onto the counter. Emilee tried to clean but was overwhelmed and left without supplies. No one cared. The laundry room resembled a dumpster. Several bags of unwashed clothes piled up untouched until the washer became unreachable. Between the clothing and dirty dishes the smell was unbearable. Emilee avoided the area and her room became her home. At thirteen years old, Emilee was on her own to feed and care for herself. Often washing her personal clothing by hand, air-drying them in her room, just to not smell of feet. The teasing may have been much worse.

"Smelly girl in 6th grade is smelly girl in 10th," said her dad when she was younger.

Her father really tried, but had no paternal or domestic skills. Their home crumbled down around them. The yardwork that they both once enjoyed went undone. Flowerbeds grew wild. Weeds eclipsed over her mother's once grand rose garden where the flowers no longer grow.

The backyard at one time was for family gatherings where they barbecued and played until the summer sun would set. Today it's a barren wasteland of broken cars and junk. The front yard, which was self-proclaimed as the greenest grass in New Haven County, appears more as a foreclosed home.

Pieces of siding flapped like a flag in the wind. He lost all interest. Emilee used to watch him pull into the driveway, exit the truck, and examine his beautiful home. When he pulls in now, his head hangs low. His wife's addiction had the same effect on him. Her father had quit.

***

November

When I was eleven, I spent my summer days home alone. My mother was here but rarely awake. I learned to dress and entertain myself and not to bother mommy.

I never answered the phone because mommy said not to.

Daddy had no clue. He left the house by six and returned when the sun was going down.

In the afternoon, mommy came out and rushed around cleaning before anyone could see the mess. She told me daddy gets mad if the house is a mess so I should never tell. I never did.

No hugs – no kisses – no love.

(EM)PTY ME

<u>EMILEE</u>

The years passed without any change. Emilee rarely saw her mother except in passing. There were never any good times, no hugs, no love. Her father did his best but lacked the tools to maintain a teenage girl. Everyday replicated the next and no one cared.

The only contact my mother and I had was through the wall which separated our cells. I listened at times, but grew tired of the same shit every night. Her life was nothing more than a prescription. She stopped loving me. I stopped loving her. It just ended. I needed her more than I needed anyone in the world and she failed. She quit- I quit!

<u>EMILEE</u>

***

<u>November</u>
<u>Thanksgiving Eve / Thanksgiving</u>

I cry at night. I want the pain in my life to end.
I'm lost. Come find me. Someone please come save me.
Please…Please…
<u>EMILEE</u>

Emilee stared at the clock, 9:34pm, counting the seconds tick away. Her curtains danced slightly with a light breeze blowing through her window. The outside was completely calm. She loved the sounds of nothing. She loved the night air and its peaceful hum. It sang her to sleep.

She awoke around midnight. Her father's voice shattered the silence. Her parent's arguments happened daily, but it was out of character for them to do it this late. It caught Emilee by surprise.

She crept toward the wall, pressing her ear against it. Her father spoke weakly. Both were crying. They argued back and forth about love and needs, life and moving on. In between moments of nothing, they cried.

"Well, where are you going?" he asked

"Away," her mother said through tears, "Just away."

"Please just stay," he begged. "I'm not ready to lose".

Her mother paused. She composed her sadness before whispering, "We already have."

The arguing stopped abruptly. He walked away and into the hallway. Emilee listened to him pace outside her door. His

- 43 -

anger increased with every step as he mumbled incoherently, searching for the right thing to say. After several minutes, he reopened their bedroom door while yelling loud enough to make Emilee back away.

"If you're going - then go!"

The door slammed. He stomped down the hall and out the front door. His truck started after several failed attempts and he pulled out in a fury - screeching his tires like a newly licensed teenager before speeding down the street and out of sight.

Emilee watched until his taillights disappeared. She cried. Always knowing that the end was near, but never expecting it to arrive, her emotions overwhelmed her.

I feel helpless and forgotten.

She obviously is leaving and my father left. My tears don't seem to matter.

Being invisible is normal, tonight I don't exist.

EMILEE

The closet doors slammed open and shut as if elephants had entered the room. The force so violent that pictures from Emilee's wall fell crashing to the floor. They hadn't spoken or seen one another in days so Emilee had no plans to intervene. Emilee stepped away from the wall. She sat on her bed, confused, afraid.

***

An hour passed, Emilee sat up in her bed rubbing her teary eyes. She reached for her headphones, placed them over her head while staring at her door - wishing it would open. Would her mother say good-bye? Emilee was unsure, but any interaction would have eased some pains. She continued to cry in silence, impatiently waiting for the end.

I tried to hide in my songs. My eyes filled with tears as I waited for it all to end. I knew she was leaving and although I hated her, I was sad. I wanted to tell her, "Stay. I love you."

I couldn't do it.

EMILEE

Emilee watched the clock numbers flip to 1am. She removed her headphones and reached for her drink on the bedside table. The house was church silent. A muted voice of Tori Amos sang through her headphones ironically about a young girl and her dad.

"I run off where the drifts get deeper -Sleeping Beauty trips me with a frown -I hear a voice you must learn to stand up- for yourself -Cause I can't always be around." ("Winter" by Tori Amos)

Her mother's door creaked opened. Emilee turned her head anticipating her walking by — however she did not. She stopped. And for a few impatient moments they both stayed mannequin still. An unmoving shadow of her feet reflected through the bottom door gap. Then the door squealed and slowly opened.

Emilee ducked beneath her sheets pretending to sleep. Her mother approached the bedside with each step marked by the floorboards squeaking. She sat on the edge of the bed, reached over and gently swept the hair from Emilee's face. Her fingers caressing her cheek in circular motions, Emilee's insides shivered. It was the first real contact in years.

"I have to go," she whispered. "I'm sorry...I failed you."

She leaned over Emilee and closed the curtain, brushed the hair from her eyes and placed a gentle kiss on her forehead which lasted a few seconds, but felt like a lifetime for Emilee.

"I love you," she said.

Her voice shook between breathes. For the first time in years, she sounded motherly – as if she cared.

The bedsprings released. Her mother placed the headphones on Emilee's head, tiptoed away, pausing before closing the door. Her footsteps lessened with distance. When the front door latched shut, Em sat up in her bed.

She wiped away the tears, reopened her curtain, and listened as the garage door beneath her engaged. The car pulled out. Emilee lifted her hand to the windows glass and waved as her mother pulled away. She never looked up.

Emilee watched her drive the opposite direction of her father. She listened until she couldn't hear her mother's broken exhaust screaming through the cold night air.

Emilee fought the regret. Why hadn't she turned around? "Stay, don't leave – I love you".

The moment passed. She slipped beneath her blankets and cried until she was asleep.

CHAPTER SIX
"A sad soul can kill quicker than a germ."
John Steinbeck

Emilee tugged on the noose. Pulling down with all her strength to test the nails she had driven into the doorframe just moments before. Once satisfied her weight would hold, she moved forward with her plan. The plan she had put into motion nearly two years prior.

She stood in the doorway staring at the rope swaying in front of her face. Her bravado was low, so she closed her eyes to relax her mind while trying to think of a happier time. After several deep breaths, she opened her eyes, stepped forward onto a milk crate and balanced it like a skateboard - rocking it side to side to test its stability. She reached for the rope, placed her head through the loop before sliding it down to her neckline like a necklace. Its tiny thread fibers brushed gently against her skin as if tiny fingers finding their grip.

Emilee grabbed the knot with her left hand while slowly tugging on the end that made it tense. The knot tightened, constricting instantly, catching her by surprise. She let out some slack and looked up, catching a glimpse of her image in the mirror hanging on the backside of her door. Emilee forced an uncomfortable smile. Her fears diminished with each completed step. She knew that it would all be over soon.

A brief feeling of accomplishment filled her body. Considering her predicament, she felt proud while scanning the room one final time.

Photos hung from her dresser mirror. Several playful images wedged between the wood and glass of friends that had come and gone throughout her years. The awards she'd earned for dance each neatly placed and shelved. The unrepaired holes in her walls the size of her fist never took her eyes from her successes -and there were many.

An award for creative writing hung proudly as if a college degree.

An award for singing in the middle school talent show and numerous ribbons for dancing all those years each placed with a purpose.

She loved animals, specifically guinea pigs.

Yet nothing could prevent this moment.

Objects she had removed an hour ago lay littered across her bed. All of her jewelry in a small-entangled pile sat surrounded by family photos. An apology note she wrote and rewrote rested perfectly creased, and sealed.

Her Notebook diaries neatly stacked against her pillows, and her favorite stuffed animal "Mr. Momo" holding a letter in his paws. A letter which her mother wrote for Emilee, several years before.

Em, my sweet,

Happy birthday to my angel - Mommy loves you so much.

Happy double digits. The age of 10 is an amazing age to laugh and smile.

I love you to the moon and beyond. I'm always here for you!!!

XOXO,
Mommy

***

Her plan to die before her 16th birthday made perfect sense. What started at 11:56pm was now 11:57pm. The seconds ticked away. She removed the suicide note from her back pocket, crumpled it in her palm (hoping it wouldn't fall out once the life had left her body.)

The two digital dots flashed with every tick, hypnotizing between its blinks.

Tick – Tick – Tick

The clock clicked forward, 11:58, two minutes from her sweet sixteen. Her last chance arrived. Having zero friends, no one was aware of her plan. No one would miss the party which nobody planned. No one would be home to miss her at all.

She glanced down at her suicide note and smoothed it out to read. The reality hit her as she re-read every word.

TO WHOM IT MAY CONCERN:

I needed to move on from this painful, stagnant life. This room, my prison cell, which I hide in everyday, has become my personal hell. Carry on as you all have the last few years. It isn't all you. Nevertheless, you are not without fault.

Good-bye,

Emilee

The digital clock blinked, 11:59. The final seconds ticked, wasting away. A red luminous light cast a digital glow on a shattered glass picture frame beside the clock. Her mother stared back through broken shards, the smile on her face seemingly growing with every blink.

CHAPTER SEVEN
"Failure is the condiment that gives success its flavor."
Capote

I often wondered if my mother thought of me as often as I thought of her. Did she ever think of me at all? Although she didn't feel my pain, the note I mailed to her last known address may help her understand.
EMILEE

Mother,
I no longer will wait for your love. You ruined us both. Do you even care? You buried us both with your selfish, miserable ways- but I'm glad you're happy now —
WITHOUT ME!

***

With a final kiss blown to her father's photo on the nightstand and a kiss to her guinea pig Peanut, she refocused. One deep and relaxing breath and her courage returned. The plan had a minute left to fulfill.

11:59:01 – 11:59:02 – 11:59:03

Emilee readjusted the rope on her neck, looked to her left, closed her eyes, swallowed and removed her legs in one quick lift. The milk crate rolled out from beneath her feet. Like two massive hands around her throat, the rope tightened. Her last breath taken, instantly escaped, and she dangled helplessly, struggling without relief like a fish on a line.

She had assumed a natural progression of airlessness would pass by pain free. There weren't many examples of survivors that told her what to expect. But Emilee couldn't have been more wrong. Within seconds, all her air was lost.

As well as she had prepared for the moment, nothing could ruin the plan. At least until the moment she found herself in now. She never had time to back out, no do overs - or excuses to put off her plan. From the second she lifted her legs and the rope constricted, she realized her mistake. Unfortunately, it was too late. Once committed to the process of hanging she had little control of how long it would take to die.

***

Sudden rushes of blood pushed directly behind her eyes. Her fingers tingled like multiple needles jabbing through their tips. Her body strained. A pain unlike anything she had ever felt shot through her spine. She attempted to take a breath. She failed.

I struggled. The rope took over my world. I have little memory of the pain. My desire and the moment, which lasted no more than a minute, I will never remember but strangely, can never forget.
EMILEE

Emilee's toes were inches away but she couldn't reach the floor. She stretched her legs with every bit of strength remaining and her natural instinct to survive, ironically, while trying to die took over the moment. The desire to breathe became stronger than that to die.

Her heartbeat slowed. Her eyes fluttered. Her body weakened - slowly dying with each decreasing beat.

Exactly how can someone describe choking? Let me try.

Remember when you were young and struggling while swimming in the deep end of the pool?

While holding your breathe on a dare for as long as you could. The neighborhood bully or your big brother pushes you further below.

As you swallow the chlorinated water and choke beneath the surface, you feel your final breathes slip past your lips.

You are drowning.

Violently, your natural impulse to live takes over. While fighting off your assailant you wiggle loose and swim breathless toward the sun, guiding you to the surface above. In a last resort of survival, you pop out of the water, flailing your arms uncontrollably. You hold onto the edge while gasping for air until your lungs refill with life and your heart rate returns.

Eventually you reach a point where you feel safe. It's just you sitting on the pool's edge shivering, wrapped in a towel and cursing your giggling aggressor.

Only here there is no ladder, no edge to grasp. You can't just slide the rope away and call timeout. There usually is no second chance. You ride through each airless moment until your final breath. The brain short-circuits and flashes past memories, fast-forwarding like a movie in your head. So vivid and so quick, appearing in a snap then suddenly going completely dark, and then gone.

EMILEE

Emilee flailed her body with her last ounce of energy. Her throat shut off and her eyes rolled back. The pain was intense. It felt as if her muscles were ripping off the bones.
Then SNAP!

***

With a graying weathered rope knotted poorly around her neck, Emilee lay unconscious on the bedroom floor. Her body weak and limp, sprawled out choking, directly below the doorframe from which she hanged.

While appreciating what she believed was her final breath turned out to be the first breathe of her second chance. With little time to understand what had happened she lay there in the dark regaining consciousness and gasping for air. She struggled with no results. All she could think was maybe, just maybe, she had crossed over.

Not quite…

This I was not prepared for. From where did they appear? From where did the voices speak?

The path I had followed which had brought me to this point has drastically changed its course. Still I was alone - or so I thought. Oxygen deprived and gasping, fighting for the thing that I despised the most. . .

My life!

CHAPTER EIGHT
"Today is yesterday's pupil."
(Franklin)

She never remembered feeling gone, as in dead. Every moment felt like a dream, and maybe it was. Truly, she never knew. What had seemed never ending could have actually been happening in seconds. It is impossible to know the length of time she lay there before they appeared.

Her eyes popped open. Lying twisted unnaturally with her arms bent wrongly behind her. She couldn't breathe. The rope tightly wrapped around her throat still constricting without relief.

The lamp on her nightstand provided the only light. Everything else was black. Her image reflected in the mirror on the back of the closet door as she struggled to break free. She wasn't alone. Something or someone, a shadow, was watching in the darkness and moving closer with every blink.

Was I alive and dreaming or was I dead and caught in between?

EMILEE

Emilee tried to move unsuccessfully, her eyesight improving with each passing second. Her limbs and fingers were numb – pins and needles asleep.

The shadow moved in.

She could feel the pain from the fall but had no means to ease it. Her breathing pattern labored through with wheezes and short bursts. With every blink she refocused clearer.

The shadow moved closer.

Emilee attempted to scream — nothing came out. Her voice was broken. Slight squeals released while trying but not enough for anyone to hear. She lay there paralyzed and face-to-face with her uninvited guest.

The shadow stood beside her.

"Emilee?" was all they said.

When the air began to speak my name, I initially felt uneasy. It may have been real or from the jostling of my brain when I fell. At the time, I didn't know. I couldn't move – I couldn't scream. They surrounded me.

EMILEE

Her once empty room began to move. Swift flying shadows darkly outlined, "Ghostlike", and moving faster than she could comprehend. She wasn't scared. Initially fear never entered her mind. Nevertheless, she was confused.

Their voices multiplied screams and whispers, getting close to her before darting away into darkness. There was an endless bright white hole in the bedroom wall where the shadows disappeared as fast as they appeared. The voices continued. Emilee closed her eyes and wished them away, but when she reopened them, nothing had changed.

They chanted repeatedly over one another. Between their flight and multiplied chatter, nothing made any sense.

"Emilee, sweet Emilee are you dead yet…are you dead?"

She wiggled violently on the floor, trying to get away. They swooped down from every angle, harassing her endlessly. Her arms couldn't move. She wanted desperately to cover her ears and hide from the voices. Emilee could only lie on the cold floor. There was no escaping their constant torture nearly driving her insane.

After several minutes of chaotic flight, all of the shadows stopped flying. Most of them hovered inches from the floor midflight, while others stood unmoving. All of them stared down. Their eyes never turned away or blinked. Emilee tried to move but could not. She tried to scream and still nothing came out.

Although they remained frozen in place, I could still hear them whispering my name. "Emilee – Emilee," they cried out in pain. Others simply laughed. Not laughs as if something were funny but the laugh of a lunatic.
EMILEE

***

The wall opening widened releasing a bright light. One single shadow flew forward, hovering, directly toward Emilee. The other shadows flew chaotically - circling, dropping into a pile on the floor, dissolving one by one before seemingly melting through the floorboards.

The single shadow moved closer. Emilee locked her eyes and attempted to scream. Still nothing came out. She could see the shadow as a girl, albeit, transparent (A ghostly image with a shredded white dress.)

Her long dark hair flew back as if the wind was at her face. She smiled.

Something about her shined brighter. She floated above me as if evaluating a crime scene. Her ghostly image moved from side to side like a boat on the ocean. Then she spoke. "My name is Neira", she said.
  EMILEE

Neira knelt down, caressing Emilee with her glowing fingers. Everything about Neira was lifelike. Her deep green eyes gave a secure feeling of calm. A glow outlined her human form, but she remained transparent. Although, the shine dimmed as seconds passed.

When she first appeared to me, she wasn't a girl – just a thing. Her movements were ghostly. Nevertheless, I trusted her. (I had no choice).
  EMILEE

***

The other shadows reappeared, surrounding Emilee's body. They never spoke. Their hands caressed her from head to toe with gentle touches over her numb body - prodding her without pain.

"Help – someone help me".

But no words transpired. A hand muffled her mouth and the noose tightened around her neck. Neira with a finger to her lips gently whispered, "No."

A sudden chill filled the room. Most of the shadows stood statuesque behind Neira, their hands holding the end of the noose. While the others continued to poke childlike at her skin.

Their eyes were cold, transparent perfect circles, blue orbs of nothing, which I could see right through. They just stared down at me. Although I wanted to, I couldn't look away. I tried to scream. I could hear the words in my head still nothing came out of my mouth.
<u>EMILEE</u>

In a quick and swift movement, all of the shadows removed their hands from her body. The void in the wall opened and each one flew through, disappearing into darkness. The wall returned as if never moved. The plaques and pictures placed exactly as before and undisturbed. The radio turned on, bouncing station to station. As if the plug pulled from the wall, the electricity abruptly turned off. Everything went dark. Their whispering, haunting voices still circled above her clearly, although distant, eventually ending in a menacing cry, "EMILEE."

The one single light on the nightstand clicked on. It was just enough to see Neira smile. Her transparent arm extended out to Emilee. Emilee struggled, but eventually reached back toward Neira. Their fingers clasped together.

"I have a specific job," said Neira.

.

"Will you come with me?" she asked.

Emilee nodded.

I wanted to speak but I had no voice. I don't even know why I nodded yes. In the moment, she made me feel at ease.
<u>EMILEE</u>

Neira floated above Emilee, her glow brighter than when she entered, before landing beside her. She picked up the rope by the broken end and studied the strands with an amusement.

"How old is this rope?" she asked beneath her grin.

Neira put both her hands beneath Emilee's body, lifting her effortlessly to her feet. She held on until Emilee had a clean stance.

The room had changed. A different type of light cascaded down from above them. Emilee achingly tilted skyward, and noticed the ceiling was gone. The open sky with all the stars shined brightly down on them.

"We have to go," said Neira.

Neira held her by the arm as if assisting an elder woman cross the street. Nothing about her, beyond her outlined glow, appeared malicious. Her beauty was evident, her intentions not so much. Emilee walked slowly, her legs still weak.

The voices of the shadows, who moments ago had been screaming, were gone. Only white noise and the whoosh of her noose dragging behind them remained.

Together, Emilee and Neira walked towards the wall with the broken rope dragging behind them. The void in the wall from where Neira appeared never opened. But still they both walked through it.

CHAPTER NINE
"There's a divinity that shapes our ends, rough-hew them how we will."
(Shakespeare)

A gentle breeze blew in their faces as they walked side by side. No words spoken, their hands clutched together while moving forward in the dark. The moonlight hid behind ominous clouds. It was unseasonably cold. The uneven ground beneath them was wet. A slick path of mud and rocks swallowing every step they took.

Emilee blindly navigated the path, entrusting in Neira. She hadn't earned her trust but Emilee's choices were limited, if not few. Being a stranger in a strange land and surrounded by even stranger beings, Neira was all she had.

"Where are you taking me?" asked Emilee.

Neira didn't respond. Her eyes never left the path.

The clouds moved steady, unveiling the moonlight that let Emilee to see the forest all around them. It was beautiful, almost unreal. Thriving full leaved trees shook gently in the night's sky. Animals scurried playfully everywhere she looked.

Emilee released her hand from Neira's, stopping sudden, burying her barefoot in the cold thick muck.

"Where are we—?"

"I suggest you continue," Neira snapped, "they're never far behind."

Emilee turned back, but only for a moment. The foot impressions they left behind appeared undisturbed and the shadows had returned. Several of them moving on the forests edge like children playing a game, ducking mischievously tree to tree. Neira's pace never wavered, but she knew the shadows were close. Her handgrip increased as she tugged on Emilee's arm.

"If they get you, fight…if you lose, you are gone forever. Understood?"

Emilee nodded and increased her pace.

"Understood?"

"Yes," she said.

Eventually, the shadows fell further back or possibly hidden against the pitch-black background. Neira seemed to believe they were safe, at least for now. She lessened her grip on Emilee and looked over to her with a smile.

"Can we rest?" asked Emilee.

Neira stopped, releasing Emilee's hand. She scanned behind them and determined that they could.

"Only for a moment."

Emilee sat on a stump, breathing heavily while rubbing her eyes. Neira stayed alert.

"Where are we going? Why are you here?"

Neira glanced from back to front. She looked down toward Emilee and reached for her hand. Emilee declined.

"We have to keep moving. They are getting close"

"Not until you give me some information. I've been more than cordial to this point, but I have to know where I am. My father will worry."

Neira sat beside her.

"I'll answer one question. Go"

Emilee began to speak then stopped. She restarted and paused again.

"Ask the question Emilee. What is it you need to know?"

Emilee took a breath.

"Where am I? Am I dead?"

"That's two questions," said Neira, "but I'll answer them both"

"My question for you is do you want to be dead? It seems like a silly question, because you put the ridiculous, worn rope noose around your neck. But you fought."

Emilee looked up.

"Yes, I did want to die. But…"

"But you tried to back out. I know. I swallowed fifty pills and drank a bottle of vodka. Fell asleep, died, and here we are. So if you asked me, you died."

Emilee began to cry.

"I feel alive. I'm walking, talking….crying"

"Well, I am too."

"So, if I am dead. Where are we?"

"Right now you're on the path chosen. Where it leads you to is where it has lead every other poor me pity party guest. Happy now?"

"I want to go back."

Neira grabbed her face.

"you can't kid. You can't. The minute you dropped your neck into the noose, it was over."

"But it broke"

Emilee grabbed the broken end from the ground and waved it gently in front of Neira.

"Not because you wanted it to. Let's go now, I've answered enough"

They grasped their hands and moved steadily, neither looking back. Hours passed. The path revealed no end. They gained some distance on the shadows but their endless chatter cried out from all around. Emilee tired, her noose still dragging behind her, but she didn't dare stop.

Several voices carried with the wind, soft whimpers, painful and sad. Neira noticed Emilee's concern and broke her silence.

"There are others like you out there — others far worse off."

Her voice never changed - no fear or desperation. Even with the shadows behind us, she just moved along filled with confidence and grace.

EMILEE

Emilee shifted her gaze to a lifeless sky. A kaleidoscope of black and grey hovered above like an infinite nothing with deadness in its grasp. A muted yellow moon moved between the clouds providing enough light to see. She looked to her left. She looked to her right. Others, like her, walked their own paths, tired and downtrodden. Each one mirroring Emilee, as if connected like puppets on a string. The only differences being the path and their guides. Shadows followed them all.

***

A gentle vibration broke the silence. Neira reached into her pocket, pulling out a small black box and pushed a button, silencing the ring nonchalantly.

"What was that?" she asked.

No answer came.

"What's the box for? Please answer me."

Neira stopped walking. She looked at Emilee.

"You must have some patience. The black box will explain itself to you very soon. Remember, you chose this. Pay attention to your surroundings. Maybe, just maybe you'll find a way out."

In an instant, things changed. The moon slid behind the clouds and a stiff cold breeze began to blow. Within seconds, the breeze turned to gusts. An ice-cold rain began to fall as a soupy mist rose from the ground. Everything was dead or dying — grey and unattractive. The treetops swayed and their icy limbs broke off, like breaking bones.

Neira stopped, turned in every direction, her hair blowing wildly in the wind - Her glow now gone.

"Follow your path – disregard theirs," she shouted over the chaos.

She pointed to the distant walkers all fighting against the storm. Emilee looked around and then looked back.

"How do I-"

Neira was gone.

I remember stopping and calling out to Neira. I began to choke. My noose pulled back and my body pushed forward. The shadows caught up. Neira never answered.

<u>EMILEE</u>

Emilee stumbled and fell. She tried to stay in the open pathway, but the shadows appearing and disappearing all around her made her roll off an embankment. She landed safely twenty feet below the shadows, but they didn't slow. As she lifted herself off the ground, they were surrounding her.

She quickly scampered beneath an icy limb and looked for shelter while avoiding falling branches all around her. The shadows chased.

The icy grass was razor sharp beneath her bare feet. Emilee fell to the ground, rolling, jumped to her feet and immediately they knocked her back to the ground.

The shadows surrounded her, circling around with a gang like mentality. They tugged at her noose, shaking away the ice that had grasped onto its threads. Emilee kicked viciously, crying out curses while trying to fight them off. The shadows only laughed, and never backed off.

"Neira", she cried.

No answer — the shadows mocked her cries: "Neira, Neira… Neira, Neira."

The shadows began tearing at her clothes, ripping her shirtsleeves. Emilee crawled and attempted to escape to no avail, kicking wildly to fight them off. She eventually collapsed beneath the mist too tired to fight any longer.

They grabbed her roughly by the arms, and swung her weary body side to side. Emilee contemplated playing dead but she didn't think it would work. She chose to quit. She lay back against the wet ground and stared up to the sky. The kicks kept coming. Sudden jerks from the noose nearly removed her head from the neck. Each time, Emilee kept staring up.

The swirling winds displaced debris from the dying landscape. Stinging rain still fell from the sky. Emilee's clothing soaked through as they dragged her beaten body through the tall grey grass.

For the next thirty seconds they abused her. She bit her bottom lip. It was all she could do to stifle her cries as her backside slid ragged over the rocks and limbs. Pain shot through her spine. The skin on her back tore open. Within seconds of unconsciousness, the shadows slammed her beaten body against a tree and fled, leaving her to die.

Emilee gasped. Her body rested ragged, slumped against a tree. The storm subsided. Everything in her sight line was dead. Between the beating and the noose, she could barely breathe. Her throat burned. The wound above her left knee bled freely. For the slightest moment, the sky was clear.

I could hear the crying all around me. The mist remained. Brown syrup like liquid poured out as if bleeding from the trees. As fast as it puddled around my legs, it disappeared.
EMILEE

The winds returned. Strong, fierce gusts blew through the deadness. The trees began to fall. Their roots ripping from the dirt as if only placed there unplanted. Branches crashed to the ground all around her, twig debris shattering on impact like glass.

Emilee pulled at the noose beneath her chin. She desperately needed air into her lungs. She tried to stand but the pain wouldn't allow her. Instead, she buried her face with her hands, protecting it from the falling and windswept debris.

The shadows were gone but their voices cried out. She peeked between her fingers. The sky above weaved a spectrum of greys, which twisted the treetops, bending them until they touched the ground. A dark cloud tore through the woods and headed straight toward her.

She blinked and it was upon her. There was no time to react.

The last thing I remember were the shadows rushing toward me at an unbelievable speed. I don't remember the impact. I don't recall the pain.
EMILEE

CHAPTER TEN
"He who doesn't fear death dies only once."
Giovanni Falcone

When I awoke, I was in a different place. It wasn't the forest or my home.

EMILEE

Her back rested against a rock wall. The bleeding had stopped but the pain remained. She was achy and sore. Puddles formed on the uneven concrete floor soaking through the backside of her tattered jeans. A strange wetness seeped through the cracks of the wall, flowing down as clear water before turning into a black mossy growth on the floor. She managed to move to her left to avoid its snail-paced flow until her only option was to stand — so she did.

Others passed by her like blind wanderers unaware of their plight. They stepped passed her without making contact, avoiding her noose stretched out onto the path. Emilee examined her wounds. She grabbed her broken rope to lessen the drag. It was soaked through. A thick, black liquid, like molasses dripped from the frayed ends.

She looked first to her left and then to her right. A poorly lit corridor stretched as far as her eyes could see in both directions. The ground had the same feel as the forest's path where her feet sank with every step. She changed her stance until finding solid ground and slowly moved toward the left.

After several minutes of walking, a light at floor level dimly escaped from beneath a door. She cautiously approached it, stood on her toes, cleared the dust from the foggy window with her palm, and pressed her face against the glass.

The room resembled a prison cell. A single chair with a swaying, flickering light bulb above it was all she could see. From the dark, far corner a shadow moved. Emilee pulled back fearing the worst, before a young man with mid-length dirty blonde hair stepped out. He sat down in a chair with an unplugged guitar on his lap, unaware of Emilee's presence. His hair draped over his eyes. He never looked up.

With her full attention to the room, a passerby knocked her from her stance. She turned. They were face to face. He never spoke. His steps were slow and heavy and a shadow stood beside him whispering in his ear. Emilee followed his empty eyes as he followed hers, while his noose dragged behind him like a puppy on a leash.

"Neira says to go in," said his voice, but his mouth never moved.

A feeling of responsibility came over me. With all the selfish reasons to worry about myself, I couldn't resist. I reached for his shoulder and he turned. His face had changed.
EMILEE

His eyes revealed pain. He wept as a child who is injured or tired. The emptiness that she saw just seconds prior had changed to human emotion.

"How can I help you?" she asked.

He stopped. The shadow tugged on his rope, snapping his head back, but he didn't flinch. He relieved some pressure with his fingers where the rope met his neck. His arm lifted and he pointed down the corridor.

"Help yourself."

Emilee turned. A funnel cloud of shadows rushed down the corridor, shattering the bulbs in the light fixtures as they furiously moved toward her. Remembering her previous run in with them, she reached for the door handle, pulling with all her strength. It wouldn't move.

Emilee pounded on the door, screaming for help. The young man inside the room pressed his face to the glass. With his empty eyes peering aimless, and a menacing smile slobbering on the glass, she looked away.

The shadows closed in, the corridor darkened with each extinguished bulb. She closed her eyes, found the handle, and pushed, crashing her full weight until the door opened. After slamming it shut, she slinked her backside against it to catch her breath.

Emilee spoke through deep inhales.

"Thank you for helping"

No response.

He sat in the wooden chair and his guitar resting on his knee. With his hair draped back over his face and struggling with the chords, he whispered to himself unhappily. His fingers moved anxiously over its rusty strings. Nothing he played was in tune, clearly frustrating him further.

Emilee followed the wall to the back corner, cleared a space on the bench and sat. She neatly stacked his blank sheets of music beside her. "Untitled — Music by: unknown" written on every piece.

Scanning the room, she took notice of empty picture frames hanging suspiciously on every wall. The room was cold. Its walls were damp and stained gray, with a mossy growth that grew from floor to ceiling, creeping between the gaps of the rocks. The guitar playing stopped sudden.

He looked up, flipping his dirty blond surfer hair from his eyes. The guitar rested beside him on its stand. He pulled out a cigarette from behind his left ear, examined it, and crossed his legs. His lips grasped the filter end, sucking inward with quick bursts until the match burned out. With his first inhale, he leaned back, his eyes fluttering and relaxed.

"Tragic, huh?" he said while exhaling and making rings of smoke.

Emilee stayed silent. She wasn't sure that he was speaking to her. She chose to sit quietly until the silence became uncomfortable.

"My names —"

"Emilee," he interrupted, "I know. I'm aware of who you are… nice noose by the way – I'm KC."

A slight grin escaped behind his puff of smoke. Emilee faked a smile back. He ignored it and grabbed his guitar.

His cigarette dangled dangerously from his lips with the ash burned down to the butt. He pinched his fingers on the filter end, inhaled a final puff, and flicked it into the corner behind him blindly, where it landed perfectly in a pile of others.

He began to strum. Every chord sounded perfect and his hums produced an actual song. The light above him reflected brightly off his now shiny guitar. The strings no longer rusted.

He appeared both happy and content with his head bouncing in a soulful rhythm while strumming perfect chords.

"The music makes me happy," he said.

Emilee grew comfortable. The room warmed and her safety appeared secure.

"You're a musician?" she asked.

"At times, I guess. But I really don't know."

The young man exhaled. A vibration sound buzzed softly. He stopped playing the guitar, fidgeted in his chair nervously, and located a small black box on the ground beside him. Emilee recognized it. It was the same as Neira had moments before they lost contact.

Nonchalantly, he pressed a button, silencing it. The guitar appeared limp in his hands. His eyes looked over toward Emilee and he shrugged his shoulders before placing his guitar's body between his feet. His expression changed. Sadness appeared.

"Close your eyes," he said.

"Why KC...you're scaring me."

"Please trust me, you're about to be very scared I'm afraid"

There was one gentle breath as he opened his mouth, biting down on the headstock. His dirty blond hair fell helplessly around his face. The guitar was no longer a guitar.

.

Emilee confused and uncertain leaned back, closing her eyes. She knocked his papers to the floor, bent over to pick them up as a single gunshot fired.

Emilee dropped to the floor, her hands cupping over her ears, eyes shut tight. A high-pitched pierce filled her head but she didn't have the courage to look. The smell in the room changed, gagging her.

"K.C. – K.C.", she shouted.

No answer came or she just couldn't hear him.

Emilee opened her eyes. The air was thick; she couldn't see him through the dust that had formed where he was sitting. She stood and blindly walked toward him, pausing when her left foot felt wetness.

The room began to clear. She looked down and watched a blood river flow over her toes, puddling around her heel. Emilee jumped forward. She hopscotched until it was useless - settling her bare foot back on the ground. While sinking it into a warm puddle that turned her stomach, she noticed KC.

She darted toward him. Her feet splashing through the blood, but she ignored it. When she reached KC, he was gone. What remained of his head rested bent back and looking up. His eyes remained open but unmoving– no life. A dark red stain resembling modern art splattered onto the stone behind him, and small traces of brain slid snail-like from the wall, dropping in a puddle on the floor.

Emilee balled up on the floor. Her hands covered over her eyes while she shook helplessly, staining her clothing in his blood. "This isn't real. This isn't real," she repeated.

Her eyes kept peeking up toward KC. Everywhere she looked had pieces left behind. His skull chunks spread throughout like broken seashells on the beach.

Her first impulse was to run. She rose to her feet, slipping numerous times, and moved toward the door. Emilee reached for the door handle while fighting the urge to look toward KC. The blood was everywhere she couldn't avoid it. Her hair dripped slow, thick droplets. Her hands left imprints on everything touched.

She began to turn the knob. Several shadows gathered at the small glass window, forcing her back. Both of her options were bad. Either face the shadows or stay in the room with a dead man. The music began to play. Emilee turned slowly.

"So many people choose a noose over the gun. I never understood it," he said while strumming.

Emilee cautiously stepped back. As alive as he appeared his head wound remained. Emilee tried not to stare as blood pushed out where the bullet entered. Yet, still he played his song.

"People underestimate a good suicide," he continued, "don't know what they're missing."

Emilee went back to the corner, hesitant and aware of everything around her. She kept her eyes on KC, using her hand to locate the bench.

"So what's your story?" he asked. "Why are you here?"

Emilee didn't answer. Her mind raced through ways of escaping.

"What is your story?" he asked again less politely.

She gathered herself, sat on the bench, watching the last bit of residue drip from the wall behind him.

"What?" she softly murmured.

Her ears still buzzed from the gunshot. She couldn't gather her nerves. A pit in her stomach wanted out but she swallowed deep and rerouted it back down.

"Why are you here Emilee, why are you...how do I say – dead?" KC. said calmly.

"Where exactly is here?" she replied still shaky.

He ignored her. He was beginning to struggle with his guitar again and its strings dulled at first and then began to rust.

"Why am I here?" she continued, "Well for one my parents forgot me, and I guess I had to escape. I have no friends, no mother...no, I don't know. No reason to stay"

KC smirked, shaking his head.

"Tragic," he said. "Sad, pitiful, blah blah blah – "

He hit a sad chord, puffing out his lip and saddening his eyes.

Emilee responded aggressively, "Well, what's your story? Why are you here? Why are you d - dead?"

He seemed amused by her question, brushed back his hair and cleared his throat. The wound in his head had closed. No blood or remnants remained. Even the wall behind him showed no signs of splatter. Emilee never even noticed it disappearing. Her eyes were fixated on his aging guitar.

"I don't know who or what I was...or what I would have been. I only know my end."

Emilee readjusted in her seat. His words, although poetic and well said, made little sense.

"Well, what about what just happened - The blood, the gun. What about this right now?"

"They call me K.C. and that's what I am — a musician ..." he pondered, "possibly."

Emilee disconnected from the conversation. Her eyes welled up with tears. She tensed her fists into tight balls and pressed the knuckles into her temples, mumbling nonsense.

"I just want to go home KC. – I need to get home"

"You are home Emilee. This is what you wanted. You tied the noose, you wrote the note"

K.C. stood from his chair and stepped toward her. He circled beneath the single hanging bulb and thought of what to say.

"I want to go back, how do I get back home?"

"You can't Em...you CAN'T." he said.

K.C. was angered. His arms flailed with his words, his face tense and reddened.

"I see people like you every day." He shouted, "I don't send invites, but still they arrive. Did I open the door? No...Yet, still, you entered."

Emilee cried. She buried her head and began slapping her own face. The shadows outside began repeating her words.

"I want to go home. I want to go home."

"Shut up, shut up – shut up," she snapped toward the door.

K.C. approached her, grabbed her by the shoulders and forced her up.

"Everyone wants to be something, Em. Some of us choose less. You chose this."

"You – chose - this," he repeated.

K.C. began shaking. He stepped back from Emilee and turned, resting his head against the mossy wall.

"You have to go. I can't help you anymore." He barked.

Emilee gathered her nerves and calmed her crying.

"Please K.C. please…please tell me how to go home."

"Go!" he yelled out, "Going home isn't an option."

His black box began to buzz again. KC didn't react. Emilee walked over and picked it up, attempting to shut it off. She flipped it in her hands but couldn't find any buttons.

"It only works for me," he said.

Emilee walked over to him and held it in front of his face. He smacked it away. Emilee picked it up, grabbed KC by his hair and shoved the box in his face.

"Tell me. Tell me now"

Emilee was angered.

KC took it from her, pressed the button and shut it down.

"You know what happens in a few minutes."

"Yes, I know. Can you please just explain it? I've been pretty calm considering I've received no answers."

Emilee grabbed at her noose.

"My body has been beaten, chased through the woods by unknown shadows. I never asked for this."

He sat in his chair and grabbed his guitar.

"We all have a black box. It alarms us to re-die. And yes, maybe this is exactly what you asked for. Maybe, before you set to kill yourself, you should have thought better."

"Re-die? Like your suicide?" she said.

"Yes. Every day – anytime, you never know when…but since mine just went off, stick around if you want."

- 82 -

KC put the guitar between his feet. He pointed.

"That's your box by the door."

Emilee walked over and examined it before picking it up. Her hand locked around it. She tried to release it unsuccessfully. It stuck to her hand.

"Don't lose it Em. That's an even worse pain than re-dying."

The door creaked open. Emilee cautiously stepped back, fearing the shadows.

Neira walked in.

"Neira," She said,"…I want to go."

Neira grabbed Emilee's hand.

"Where did you get that?"

"KC said it was mine."

Neira angrily marched toward KC, kicking his guitar from between his feet. He looked up giggling.

"I never told her to grab it. I simply said it was hers."

Neira smacked him. She grabbed a fistful of his hair, pulling him close. She whispered into his ear.

"Ok, ok…let go - I know, I know and I will." He said.

Neira released him and walked over toward Emilee. KC stumbled on his words before gathering what he wanted to say.

I remember it because every day I re-live it," he said, "You will, too Em"

Emilee looked toward him.

"What"

"You asked me my reasons, of why I was here. I am here because, like you, I made a choice. Maybe if you're lucky – you'll get another chance."

He put the body of his guitar back between his feet. Neira put her arm around Emilee and guided her toward the door.

"I'm not afraid of dying. Total peace after death," he yelled out, "becoming someone else is the best hope I've got."

Emilee peered back before exiting. KC. lowered his mouth onto the headstock. He raised his hand and waved her away toward the door as if shooing away a fly.

She understood and continued out the door.

The door slammed shut and a lock engaged. Emilee grabbed Neira's hand and stepped into the empty hall, looking in each direction. With their first step, they heard the gun shot. She didn't look back. Emilee knew the result. Before she was too far away, his guitar began to play, the last thing she heard was his song.

K.C. found his hum. His lyrics came to life.
"If you knew this was your only chance — would you think it through again — if you take it — then take it — and know you always can.

Make another day your gem — take the opportunity as they open — and take my friend and take and live again."

Neira suddenly halted. She took Emilee and whispered in her ear. Emilee looked confused but nodded in agreement. Neira pointed her to the left and she turned and went right.

Emilee alternated between watching each step and looking back toward Neira. Eventually she saw nothing but darkness in both directions. She continued to follow the path that Neira pointed out. Albeit, fearful and overwhelmed.

CHAPTER ELEVEN
"Moving on is a simple thing, what it leaves behind is hard." Dave Mustaine

Neira moved quickly through the corridors. She was comfortable in the environment and knew her way around. Her plan had a low probability but it was the first, and possibly the only opportunity she would have to let her father know to carry on. It had to work.

She approached the split in the corridor. If she went left, she'd get where she needed quicker but would dangerously pass through the "bottom". The bottom roamed free, no doors. They're the ones that accepted their fate of staying. In most cases, they had no one left behind that missed them, but they also had specific jobs to fulfill. The type of jobs that cause harm to anyone they chose; including the guides who share the space.

She reached into her pocket and peered at her little black box. Neira went left once she saw the numbers tick away. She only had 33 minutes before her re-dying.

***

Emilee wandered the corridor peering through every door she passed. All but one had no vacancy. She spent as little time watching them as possible. Partly fearing the shadows closeness, and partly just plain fear was enough to move her forward. Luckily, the ones she did watch never re-died in those moments.

Just as K.C. had with her, each room had a person reliving their death. All calmly speaking like a teacher in classroom.

Emilee didn't watch the process but she couldn't help hearing each painful, final moment. She covered her ears but the screams still found their way in. Her pace increased with her need to escape, moving through the corridor with only two things on her mind; finding Neira and a way back home.

***

The ground remained the same; wet and unsteady. The air temperature changed. In fact, it was hot, as if a fire was burning uncontrolled. She could feel the heat and smell the air as it increasingly worsened. It wasn't the smell of a warming fire, not hotdogs or chicken like the one she remembered from her father's barbecues, but more like rotting garbage. It forced her to gag. She paused to pull her shirt up to over her face to act as a mask. It didn't help.

The glow of flames reflected through a door up ahead. Smoke escaped slowly and the increasing odor in the air was god-awful. Screams of agonizing pain filled the corridor. The kind you run to and assist if heard in the outside world. Emilee stopped, looked in both directions — no one behind her, no one in front of her. At the very least, the fire gave her light while behind her the unknown of the darkness was waiting. She moved ahead cautiously and with the intent of helping.

She reached the door and considered her plan of action. The fire was so hot that just being close to it burned the uncovered skin on her body. There were no alarms, no extinguishers or others to help. She yelled into the room numerous times and received no response.

Emilee wrapped her hand in her shirt and reached toward the handle.

"Don't," shouted Neira, slapping her above the wrist to knock her hand from the handle.

"They need to burn."

Emilee grabbed her and hugged her tight. Neira had scratches on her face like she walked through a rose bush.

"But they're screaming — they can see us."

Two teenaged boys in black trench coats stared out toward Em and Neira. The flames chased them as they ran hopelessly end to end - both of them in a panic, stripping off their clothing as it set aflame.

"Like everyone you have seen these two took their lives."

Neira spit in their direction. It hit the outside of the glass and boiled in an instant. She smiled. Their desperate faces showed while running toward the door.

"Unfortunately, they took others. Others who were innocents…"

The fire intensified along with their screams. Their fists pounded desperately against the glass, staining it with blood on impact before bubbling on the window like butter in a preheated pan.

Emilee looked away from their faces as they suffered and burned. Their skin shed and charred, dripping away from their bones like candle wax before engulfing both of them into nothing.

Neira guided Emilee away before seeing the two young men re-ignite. The intensity of the heat lessened as they moved further from the door but the screams continued.

Emilee looked back; in a bold flash, the room lit up then darkened. The screaming stopped.

"Who are they?" asked Emilee.

"Eric Harris and Dylan Klebold - ," she said.

Neira had no remorse. In fact, she seemed amused to see them suffer. She had an energy renewed as if the burning entertained her.

They stopped once safely distant from the heat. Emilee lifted her noose and leaned against the rocks. Neira remained alert.

"Those two scums planned a mass shooting. They cowardly ambushed their fellow students, purposely killing innocents." Neira smiled, "And now they burn, burn, burn…every hour, every day."

***

Neira's black box buzzed, as did Emilee's. They both looked down at their box.

Neira shrugged her shoulders and pulled Emilee closer to her.

"You had options Emilee, but you chose death. I did the same."

Emilee wiped her eyes. Neira helped her and brushed away the hair from Emilee's eyes.

"Your box is going to open. Where it takes you now won't be pleasant. Eventually you'll adjust."

"You mean I re-die?"

"I'm sorry Em."

Emilee gathered her emotions and stood up. They both held each other tight.

"I have to move on," Said Neira.

"Will I see you again?"

"You will, but sadly we won't recognize each other. My guide services have expired. We start over."

Neira's black box alarmed.

She released Emilee from her hands and pulled out a letter from her pocket.

"Take this," Neira said, before walking away.

Emilee stuffed it into her front pocket and waved until Neira was out of sight, her glow returning as she entered the dark.

Emilee's black box alarmed.

Shadows rushed out toward her from every angle. The wall cracks bled the black, syrupy liquid that fell to the floor and grew into shadows. She had no time to run, and they surrounded her. Her eyes closed as she took one deep breath, as she did in her closet, just to calm her nerve. She wasn't afraid.

Several shadows grabbed her frayed end of the noose, and wrapped it around the ceiling beam above her, hoisting her up. The noose tightened but didn't choke. They held her legs beneath her.

Emilee didn't beg for forgiveness. She didn't speak.

One shadow looked up at her. Emilee locked in on its eyes.

"You'll get used to this," they said to her," Ready, one – two…"

Then all went black.

CHAPTER TWELVE
"A mistake is simply another way of doing things."
Katharine Graham

Emilee walked alone. The rock structure returned to the path like the one she followed in, except the forest now had life. The stars shone bright and the birds flew free against the clear night sky. Gentle winds blew through healthy leaves and the trees stood steady in their roots. The world returned to all its beauty, all its pleasures, and all of its wonder - all of the things that Emilee forgot.

A tear formed in her eye.

Neira's voice blew through the warm breeze.

"What you believed would solve your problem was wrong."

"I know," she said to no one.

"Don't ever forget the rooms. Don't ignore the lessons."

Emilee watched a group of birds fly toward her, swooping and playing. Emilee followed them until they were specks against the bright sky.

"They are beautiful aren't they Neira?"

No reply, Neira was gone.

Emilee continued on the open, dry path, with her noose still in tow. There were no shadows — No dark stormy skies, no fear. She walked as far as her legs would take her before resting against a tree.

She resumed her journey. After a few hours, the sky brightened. Emilee watched the sunrise from behind a hillside. Another beautiful moment she had forgotten. She paused briefly and just watched it.

In the distance her home appeared. Emilee wrapped the noose around her arm and ran as fast as she could. Once there, she cautiously touched it to convince herself she was home.

She stood beneath her bedroom window. The temperature chilled but rays of sunshine still cascaded through the treetops. She felt safe. She was home.

Emilee walked to the front of the house. It wasn't there. The sky darkened with each step, every corner she turned brought her back to beneath her bedroom window.

She stood confused, staring out into the forest. Neira spoke. The sun disappeared.

"If you want it, wish it. But if you don't walk back."

"Can I stay with you?" asked Emilee.

"No"

"Go home Em," she said.

Emilee turned her face to the house. She placed both hands on it and closed her eyes. Every memory flashed through her mind.

Her mother leaving, the kids at school.

No friends. The pain – the depression.

Then she saw the small things, like the moment she stepped on stage and danced as a child. She saw a smile on her mother's face. Emilee ran, laughing wildly, before her father tossed her into a large pile of leaves.

"I want to go home, I want to go home."

CHAPTER THIRTEEN
"Everything has beauty, but not everyone sees it."
Confucius

Emilee struggled on her bedroom floor. Her vision blurred. She shook her head trying to regain her eyes while stretching her fingers for feeling. Her vision returned. The room was dark with a distant blinking red light flashing against the wall. Her room unchanged.

She pushed herself up from the floor and walked toward the bed. All the jewelry, photos and notebooks rested untouched, unmoved. The house was silent. Emilee looked over to the clock. How long was she gone? She didn't know.

Everything seemed as a dream. The noose was gone as well as the nails. She could breathe without restrictions and her body appeared unharmed. The broken picture of her mother was no longer shattered. Emilee turned on her light and felt her neckline, looking in the mirror and noticed no marks.

I remembered Neira and my trip to the other side. I remember preparing my death. I remember the images I saw and I remember the pain inflicted. Maybe I dreamt it. Maybe it never happened. EM

Emilee sat on the bed and gathered her notebooks. She placed her jewelry on her dresser, admired her photos, turned on the radio, grabbed her stuffed animal and wept.

"Neira?" she whispered. No response spoke back. She never expected her to, but felt like she had to try.

Spreading out her blank notebooks around her, she began to write. Hours passed but she filled three completely with her journey. Where she was, how she felt, a shorthanded version but legible at least to her. She stacked them in with her previous notes and placed them beside her bed.

Emilee changed into her sweatpants, emptying her pockets before throwing her clothes into the corner. The note was in her hand, written on paper antiquated and fragile. On the outside fold, Neira wrote "For Daddy", with an address beneath it. Emilee placed it on her nightstand before closing her eyes. Before she knew it, she was dreaming.

***

When Emilee awoke, it was nighttime. She had slept through the day. Unaware of it being her sixteenth birthday, she stretched while yawning, turned on her stereo, and walked toward her door to use the bathroom. Something stopped her. Her eyes turned to the radio. She listened. The chords rang out and she recognized the song. A new song – a first time premiere by a Connecticut band Fear the State.

She listened closely as the song played - The same song that KC sang when she closed his door.

Emilee stood motionless in the doorway leaning against the wall. The song played but was secondary in the moment. She thought of Neira, she thought of KC, she thought of the people in the forest who had suffered by their own hands. She remembered the shadows dragging her through the darkness. It was real, not a dream. When the vocalist sang, the words were real.

"If you knew this was your only chance — would you think it through again? — if you'd take it — then take it — and know that you always can."

Emilee ran to the kitchen, found a notebook and paper, scribbling a quick note before running back to her room. She threw her notebooks into a gym bag and dressed. She remembered the note from Neira, and tossed it in her bag.

She began out the door, grabbed her Dad's spare keys and saw it was raining. She took a raincoat from the closet and ran to the car.

Emilee struggled with the keys but eventually figured it out and backed out slowly. She didn't have a license but had driven enough to get by. She was only going down the street.

***

She arrived at 22 Acacia avenue and got out of the car, leaving it running. Walking slowly through the rain and onto the front porch, she knocked three times.

The house appeared empty. She looked into the window and saw a flickering light but no one around. She knocked again, this time harder. A voice yelled out. Emilee contemplated running but waited patiently.

After a few minutes, she gave up, knocked three more times before walking away, placing the bag against the lamppost. Her shoes sunk into the lawn just like the path she followed Neira on. She wasn't afraid. Emilee opened the car door, got in and drove off. She never looked back.

The rain had stopped when she pulled into her driveway. The porch light was on. She parked the car, locked it and went inside, hanging her father's keys back on the key holder. Quietly she walked down the hallway and stood outside her father's door. The TV was on. She turned the knob slowly and gently pushed open the door. He was asleep, tightly wrapped in his covers, snoring like a chainsaw on full throttle. He had a gift wrapped crudely at the foot of his bed.

She smiled. He looked at peace with the past. Emilee closed the door and retreated to her room.

Emilee awoke to her alarm, hit the snooze and repositioned toward her window. Beams of sunlight filled her room forcing her eyes back open. The breeze blew through the window, sending a morning chill up her spine. She was happy.

***

Her father sat reading the paper and sipping his coffee. He acknowledged Emilee with a nod and offered her breakfast.

"Sit Emilee, let's chat."

Emilee sat with a suspicious mind. Her father rarely spoke, not to mention to her.

"Life going okay?"

"Ummm, yea…I guess," said Emilee, "is everything okay with you?"

He neatly folded his paper and removed his cheater glasses.

"I'm sorry I missed you on your birthday yesterday. I was visiting a friend in the hospital, came home, and you were asleep the whole day."

" Didn't feel well." She said while pouring syrup over her breakfast.

"Everyone deserves a second chance Em"

Emilee didn't understand his comments but she still nodded and smiled. Emilee was so busy stuffing French toast into her mouth she was unaware he was pointing to a gift on the table.

When her father pointed, this time animated, Emilee looked again. She leaned back in her chair.

"What is it?" she asked nervously.

"Open it up."

Emilee reached for the gift, first reading the card that was taped to gift. She began to cry.

"Take it to your room if you want privacy."

Emilee wiped her eyes and stood up. Before going, she embraced her father and whispered in his ear.

"Thank you."

Her father hugged her back.

"You're welcome."

***

Emilee lay in her bed. Her stuffed animal "Momo" held tightly in her grasp. She placed the unwrapped gift beside her, and unfolded the letter.

Dear Emilee,

Let me first begin with an apology. I never meant to lose control and I never intended to fail. I am getting better.

I recently checked myself into a rehabilitation center and for the first time in a long time, I am sober.

For the past few weeks, your father has been visiting. He wants us to be a family. I can't promise it will work, but I can promise I will always be your mother.

Happy sweet 16.

He tells me you've grown into a responsible young lady. I wish I could have been with you today but currently I am still unable to leave.

Mom xoxo

The letter continued. Outside her door, she heard a faint knock.

"All good kid?" said her father.

Emilee wiped her face and got up to open the door, card in hand.

"Ready to go?" he said.

Emilee was confused.

"Go where?"

Her father smiled and walked over to her bed. He picked up the gift.

"Open'er up kid, times wasting."

Emilee tore through the wrapping paper, and used her fingernail to cut the tape from the cardboard box. She pushed aside crumpled tissue paper until she was staring at her gift.

"Are you serious?" Emilee cried out.

"We are very serious. But hurry up, the flight leaves in three hours."

Emilee packed her bags and gave her guinea pig enough food and water to last three days. They arrived at Bradley Airport and awaited their flight.

"Dad"

He looked over toward Emilee and winked.

"Don't worry Em, your mother will be happy to see you."

THE END

AUTHOR'S NOTE

Of course, in the end, I could have left Emilee lost on the other side. I could have graphically written words that continued to let her suffer. But my point would have never been made.

I didn't initially intend to create a story with a lesson. I started with a vision, and let the story lead me to tell its ending.

Emilee couldn't see the beauty in the world. It took an attempt on her life to open her eyes. Although, this sounds like a nice, happy ending, it isn't an ending that in real life is common.

My intent was to scare someone thinking about suicide. I wanted to create a scenario that showed that the pain doesn't ever end.

Although, my work and characters are fictitious, maybe my story has truth. No one comes back from death, whether self-inflicted or natural. My suicide world may be real.

Who knows?

F.A. Carroll

A special thanks to Marc Amendola, Jeff Sobon and Jim Dizm. Fear The State is an actual band, and Live Again, as sung by KC in the story, is an actual kick ass song.

Find them on social media and support the music.

Thank you for reading my story. Please feel free to connect on social media.

www.FACarroll.com

Made in the USA
Las Vegas, NV
21 May 2021